Playful Pete
Cooks Up a Party!

by Janet Tomita

illustrations by Paul Hart

published by WRITERS PRESS

2

*Windows of opportunities
open wide when a parent believes
in their child's
self-worth.*

Playful Pete
Copyright © 1998 by Janet Tomita
Illustrated by Paul Hart
Published by Writers Press

ISBN 1-885101-92-9

10 9 8 7 6 5 4 3 2 1

Printed In The U.S.A.

For Louie Attebery
who taught me to
appreciate whimsical
characters.

Janet Tomita

To Sammy Boy–
You'll always make me proud
as long as you
do your best.

Paul Hart

"I'm cooking dinner," said Playful Pete.
"I'm cooking dinner tonight!"
"And what do you need my dear little sweet?"
asked Big Momma Pearl DuBright.

"Spaghetti and rye with blueberry pie,
would ever be so fine.
But Broccoli Stew all covered with goo,
might please our family of nine."

"Look for some grapes that are pleasingly plump,
and bring me some things to munch.
I must not forget to feed the pets,
the goodies they like to crunch."

"I'm cooking dinner," said Playful Pete.
"I'm cooking dinner tonight!"
"And what will you wear my dear little sweet?"
asked Big Momma Pearl Dubright.

"Plaids and stripes would be very nice,
to serve my dinner of stew.
But broccoli is green and goo is white,
so I think bright blue will do."

"Look for shoes that are very smooth,
with laces of orange and black.
A vest might be just right for me,
and would go with brand new slacks."

"I'm cooking dinner," said Playful Pete.
"I'm cooking dinner tonight!"
"And who will come my dear little sweet?"
asked Big Momma Pearl DuBright.

"A shark or two, three clams and me,
and maybe a sea horse too.
Oh dear I fear, I've run out of room,
to invite a whale that's blue."

"So drive the truck and pick up some stuff,
that will stretch this place outright!
Perhaps I can squeeze some snakes in with ease,

and sit with my mama tonight!"

More great children's books that include ALL children!

—— Enrichment Collection Set #2 ——

Becca & Sue Make Two by Sandra Haines
With practice and cooperation, *together we're better.*
Donnie Makes A Difference by Sandra Haines
Perseverance wins in this inspirational story.
My Friend Emily by Susanne Swanson
Helping through friendship and understanding.
Lee's Tough Time Rhyme by Susanne Swanson
Preparation conquers challenges.
The Boy on the Bus by Diana Loski
Understanding teaches lessons in friendship.
Dinosaur Hill by Diana Loski
Adventure without limitations.
Zack Attacks by Diana Loski
Success in spite of adversity.

—— Other inclusion-minded books ——

Eagle Feather
by Sonia Gardner, illustrated by James Spurlock
A *special edition* treasure of Native American values in stunning artwork.
Catch a Poetic Hodgepodge
by Kevin Boos, illustrated by Paul Hart
A whimsical collection of poems especially written for children.

1-800-574-1715
www.writerspress.com
WRITERS PRESS
5278 CHINDEN BLVD.
GARDEN CITY, ID 83714